This book belongs to:

_____

For Duncan and Ross

This paperback edition first published in 2013 by Andersen Press Ltd.

This edition with new illustrations first published in 2012 by Andersen Press Ltd.

First published in Great Britain in 1970 as 'The Magician who Lost his Magic'

by Andersen Press Ltd., 20 Vauxhall Bridge Road, London SW1V 2SA.

Published in Australia by Random House Australia Pty.,

Level 3, 100 Pacific Highway, North Sydney, NSW 2060.

Text and Illustrations copyright © David Mckee, 1970 and 2012.

Colour separated in Switzerland by Photolitho AG, Zürich.

Printed and bound in Malaysia by Tien Wah Press.

10   9   8   7   6   5   4   3   2   1

British Library Cataloguing in Publication Data available.

ISBN 978 1 84939 525 0

Melric
THE MAGICIAN WHO LOST HIS MAGIC

David McKee

ANDERSEN PRESS

Melric was the king's magician. Every day he carried out the king's orders. If the king wanted to swim, Melric made the sun come out. If the king was too hot, Melric made the sun go in. When he wasn't working for the king, Melric helped everybody else – all by magic. Melric was always busy. No one else was busy at all.

One morning Melric woke up late. He muttered the spell that should
have washed and dressed him and made his bed, but nothing happened.
He said the spell again, louder. Nothing happened. He shouted the
spell. Still nothing happened. In a great hurry – because the king didn't
like to be kept waiting – Melric dressed himself, making a terrible mess
of it. He took one look at the bed and left it, unmade.

The king was angry with Melric for being late. "Come along, Melric," he said. "I want this room painted. After that, there's a crowd outside and they all want things done."

Melric tried and tried and tried the spells for painting rooms but nothing happened. Gradually everybody realized what the trouble was. MELRIC'S MAGIC WAS GONE.

"What shall we do?" said the king. "Our enemies will attack us when they hear your magic cannot defeat them."

"Perhaps my sister, Mertel the witch, can help," suggested Melric. "I'll go and see her at once."

As the people began to realize that Melric couldn't help them, they tried to do things for themselves, things they hadn't done for ages. There was trouble everywhere – even simple things went wrong. Poor Melric left, feeling very sad that he was of no use.

Usually, when Melric wanted to go on a journey, he travelled by magic. This time he had to walk. All along the way he passed people trying to do things they hadn't attempted for years. Melric hurried on, hoping his sister Mertel could help him, so that he could help everybody else.

Mertel lived under an old tree in a forest.

By the time Melric arrived there, he was exhausted.

Mertel listened to her brother's story. She tried a few spells but they were useless. She made him drink an evil tasting brew but even that did not bring back his magic.

At last she said, "I can't help you. Go and see cousin Guz, the wizard. You can borrow one of my spare broomsticks to take you to his island." Melric said goodbye and flew off, grateful at least not to be walking.

Melric liked visiting Guz. Guz kept strange pets, and would often change the shape or the size of his island just for fun. Guz was pleased to see Melric, but as soon as he heard the sad story, he realized there would be no time for fun.

Guz was a first class wizard and set to work immediately with his strongest spells. In spite of wonderful bangs, and flashes galore, Melric remained as unmagic as ever.

"There's no choice," sighed Guz, "you will just have to visit the wise Kra. He can do anything. I'll get you to the bottom of his mountain by magic but you'll have to climb the rest of the way. Kra's own magic stops people from dropping in." Guz sprinkled Melric with magic powder and in a flash Melric left the island.

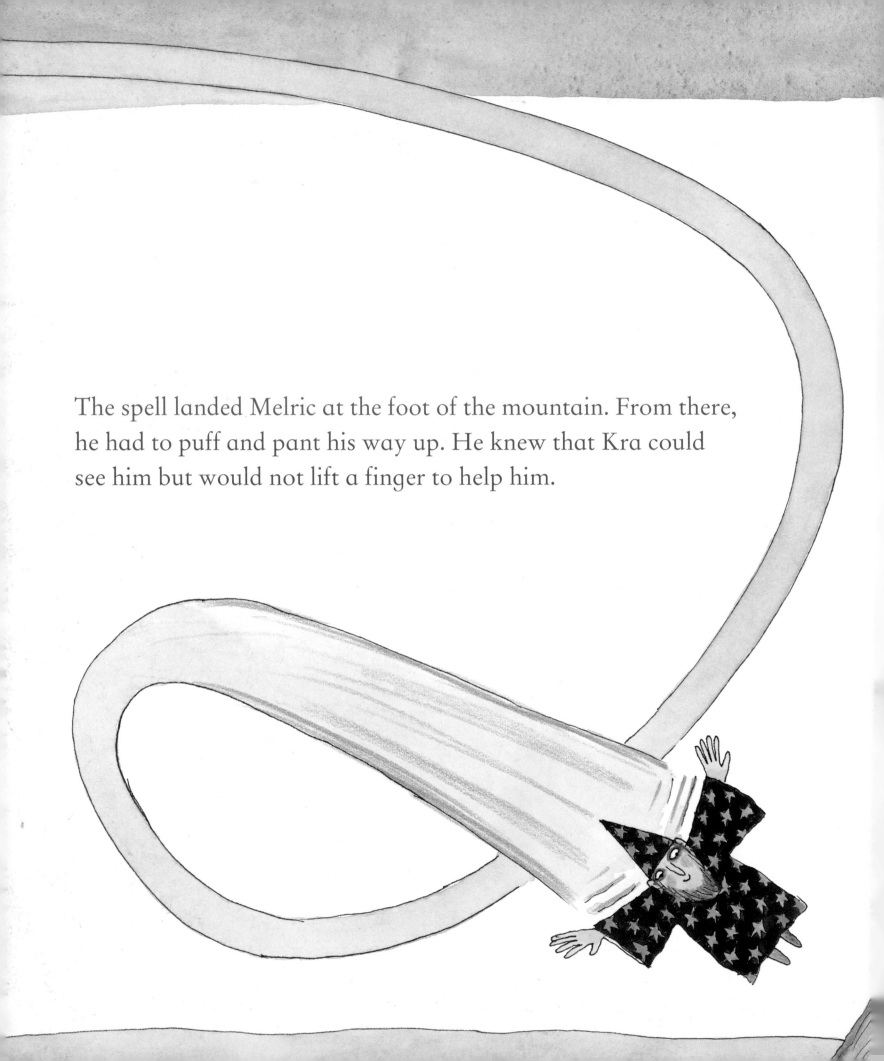

The spell landed Melric at the foot of the mountain. From there, he had to puff and pant his way up. He knew that Kra could see him but would not lift a finger to help him.

When at last Melric arrived at the top, he told Kra his story.
"You are stupid," said the old man. "You just wasted your
magic instead of helping people."
"What!" Melric almost shouted. "I've always helped
people. I've done everything for them."
"That's just the trouble," said Kra. "You've taught them to
rely on you, and when you fail them they can't do a thing
for themselves. That's not helping them."
Melric didn't utter a word. Then the wise Kra said, "This
time I'll give you back your magic, but if you waste it
again, it may be lost for ever."

Melric's toes and fingers tingled, and he knew his magic was back.

"Thank you, sir," he said. "Now I must fly." And he changed into a bird and headed for home. As he flew, he passed over Guz and then over Mertel. They recognized him even though he was a bird, and waved, happy to see that he had his magic back.

When Melric reached the castle he found that the king's enemies had launched a big attack. They had heard that the magician had lost his magic and had wasted no time in trying to seize the castle.

This is a good time for a spell, thought Melric.

The big bird landed on a turret and changed into the magician.
He held out his hands and the air was filled with a green light.

In a few seconds all the enemy soldiers were changed into black cats.

"Open the doors," called Melric. "Our dogs can chase them home. They'll change back when they get there."
The king started to thank Melric but he was promptly surrounded by a crowd of people. "Melric, mend my chair," called one, and then all at once the rest of them started asking Melric to do things. Everything was back to normal, or so the people thought.

Melric raised his hand and called for silence. "In the future you must manage without me," he said. "Magic will only be used on very special occasions. Now off you go, as I shall be very busy."

For the rest of the day everyone went happily about their business.
And Melric? Melric had to learn to make his bed.

Other books illustrated by David McKee:

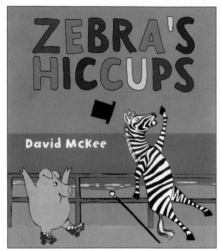

9781842709238

9781849395816

9781849393058

9781849393898

9781842704684

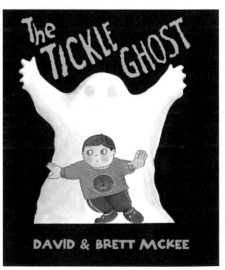

9781849392464